D1584345

22153337P

Oscar's best Friends

WITHDRAWN

Look out for other
LITTLE DOLPHIN titles:

Hattie's New House
Party Time, Poppy!
Milo's Big Mistake
Fergal's Flippers
Sammy's Secret

And if you've enjoyed reading about
Little Dolphin and his adventures,
why not try reading the Little Animal Ark
books, also by Lucy Daniels?

Oscar's Best Friends

Illustrated by DAVID MELLING

LUCY DANIELS

Hodder
Children's
Books

A division of Hodder Headline Limited

PEBBLE BEACH

HATTIE

TO PUFFIN SHORE

FERGAL

LOBSTER BRIGADE STATION

POPPY

UR
B

REEF

RAGGED ROCKS

SHIPWRECK

VINNIE

OSCAR

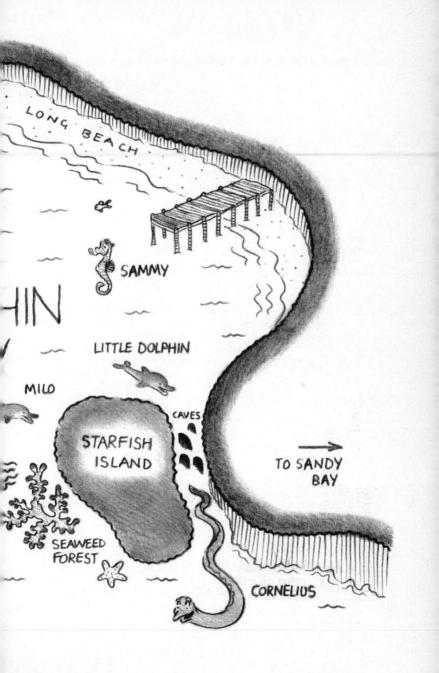

To Mackenzie Snowdon

Special thanks to Jan Burchett and Sara Vogler

Text copyright © 2004 Working Partners Limited
Created by Working Partners Limited, London, W6 0QT
Illustrations copyright © 2004 David Melling

First published in Great Britain in 2004
by Hodder Children's Books

The rights of Lucy Daniels and David Melling to be identified as the Author
and Illustrator of the Work respectively have been asserted by them in
accordance with the Copyright, Designs and Patents Act 1988.

10 9 8 7 6 5 4 3 2 1

All rights reserved. No part of this publication may be reproduced, stored in a retrieval
system, or transmitted, in any form or by any means without the prior written permission
of the publisher, nor be otherwise circulated in any form of binding or cover other than
that in which it is published and without a similar condition being imposed on the subse-
quent purchaser.

All characters in this publication are fictitious and any resemblance to real
persons, living or dead, is purely coincidental.

A Catalogue record for this book is available from the
British Library

ISBN 0 340 87349 3

Printed and bound in Great Britain by
Clays Ltd, St Ives plc

The paper and board used in this paperback by Hodder Children's
Books are natural recyclable products made from wood grown in
sustainable forests. The manufacturing processes conform to the
environmental regulations of the country of origin.

Hodder Children's Books
A division of Hodder Headline Limited
338 Euston Road, London NW1 3BH

CLACKMANNANSHIRE
F LIBRARIES 9/04

2215333 7 Φ

CHAPTER ONE

"I've had a lovely holiday at Puffin Shore!" said Little Dolphin. "But it's great to be back home!" He was rolling around in the warm waters of Urchin Bay with his dolphin friends, Milo and Poppy.

"My mum and dad took me on a Whale Express tour," chirped Poppy. "We went through Cuttlefish Cove and round Pilchard

Point – and look what I got from Walrus Lagoon." She did a twirl to show off the pretty pebble necklace she was wearing.

"Where did you go for your holiday, Milo?" she asked.

Milo thought hard. "Can't remember the name," he said at last. "But it was sunny and there were lots of waves!"

Little Dolphin grinned. Milo was such a scatterbrain. "Oscar should be home from Sandy Bay soon," he said. "I've heard it's really cool and trendy there."

"And he's bound to have lots of funny stories to tell," added Milo. "That octopus gets himself into a tangle wherever he goes!"

"I can't wait to see him!" whistled Poppy. She spun around with excitement, knocking Milo into a clump of seaweed.

"Let's play something – before Poppy spins herself into a tizzy!" Little Dolphin exclaimed, as Milo struggled out from the floppy leaves.

"I got a new board game on holiday. Wait here."

He darted off along the coral reef and into his cave, then swam back clutching the game under his flipper. "It's called Flotsam and Jetsam," he told them.

He showed his friends the board with its black and white square markings, along with a shell box of flat pebbles used to play the game. Half the pebbles were black and the others were white. "The board is made from a bit of the old wreck at Puffin Shore," he told them proudly. "Mum and I swam around it —

it's much bigger than our old wreck here at Urchin Bay."

Poppy peered eagerly at the box of pebbles and squares on the board. "How do you play?" she asked.

Little Dolphin began to explain. "One side has the white pebbles and the other side has the black—" He stopped. Someone was swimming over to them.

It was Oscar!

"Hello, Oscar!" they all called. "Welcome back!"

They waited for Oscar to lollop up to them, waving all eight arms at once. He usually tangled himself into a big slippery knot!

But today Oscar just gave one tiny cool flick of an arm.

Little Dolphin wondered what was wrong with him. He didn't seem his usual bouncy self.

"How was your holiday, Oscar?" asked Milo.

"Best ever," said Oscar casually.

"What did you do then?" demanded Poppy, spinning round him.

Oscar just shrugged.

Then Little Dolphin noticed they were being watched. Two squids were lounging on the sand nearby. They looked really cool. One was wearing a cap and the other wore sunglasses. They waved a couple of arms at Oscar.

"That's Smudge and Blot," Oscar explained proudly.

"My new friends from Sandy Bay." Smudge and Blot glided over to them, squirting out hazy clouds of squid ink.

"Give me a high eight, my friend!" called Smudge. He and Oscar swam at each other and slapped all their eight arms together. Then Smudge turned and looked at the dolphins.

"Who are these guys, Osc?" he drawled.

Osc? thought Little Dolphin in surprise. He'd never heard Oscar called that before.

"They're the friends I told you about," Oscar drawled back. "Little Dolphin, Milo and Poppy."

"Give me a high eight!" squeaked Milo, waving his flippers up and down at the squids.

"You've only got two flippers!" whispered Oscar, looking embarrassed.

"Oh yes," clicked Milo, "I forgot ..."

"So what do you all get up to, here in Urchin Bay?" asked Smudge.

"Yeah," added Blot, peering at them over his sunglasses. "What do you do for fun?"

Little Dolphin pushed his new game towards them. "I've got a new game," he chirped. "It's called Flotsam and Jetsam. You can join in, if you want."

"A board game?" said Smudge.

"Bor-ing!" said Blot.

Little Dolphin knew Oscar loved board games. But today he just looked away, as if he found them boring too. Feeling rather silly,

Little Dolphin nudged his new game under some weed.

"I know! We'll show you a dolphin tower!" said Poppy. "I'll be at the bottom." She stood on her tail on the sea-bed. Milo perched upright on her nose. Then Little Dolphin swam up and balanced on top of Milo's nose. "This is our best one yet!" whistled Poppy, trying not to wobble.

"Is that it?" asked Smudge. He didn't sound very impressed.

"No, I'm sure we can do more!" chirped Poppy. "How about a *spinning* dolphin tower?"

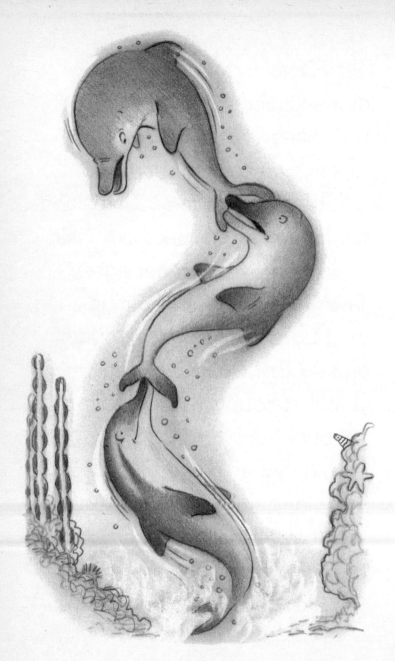

"Oo-er – do you know anything about this, Little Dolphin?" Milo squeaked up to him, sounding alarmed.

"No, I don't!" Little Dolphin called back.

Then, without a word of warning, Poppy started to spin!

There was a flurry of flippers and swirling sand – and the dolphin tower collapsed in a heap on the sea-bed!

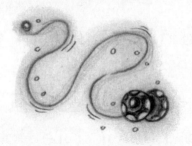

CHAPTER TWO

"We've never tried a spinning
tower before," Little Dolphin
squeaked, feeling embarrassed.

Blot shrugged, looking bored.
"We've got to liven things up
here, Smudge, my friend," he
said.

"Yeah!" agreed Smudge.
"And I know just what we need."
He flicked off his cap with one

20

tentacle and pulled out a yo-yo made of two shiny black shells with the other. "The Riptide!" he announced.

Little Dolphin, Milo and Poppy gazed admiringly at it. They all had yo-yos, but theirs were nothing like this.

"It's the best in the ocean," Oscar told them, as the yo-yo flashed round their heads. "It's even got reflector shells!"

Smudge made the Riptide whip out to the side and back, quick as a flash. "No one else can do that trick," he boasted. "I call it the Supercrab.

And now for my Electric Eel." The yo-yo wiggled through the water, flashing as it went.

"It's so *deep*!" drawled Blot.

Little Dolphin wondered what Blot meant. "It's not deep here," he explained. "The water's quite shallow near the reef. If you want deep water you have to go to …" He stopped. Smudge and Blot were laughing at him!

"You don't understand, Little Dolphin," whispered Oscar

hurriedly. "*Deep* means great or brilliant. It's trendy talk in Sandy Bay."

Little Dolphin felt *very* silly now. He almost wished a giant clam would come and swallow him up.

Smudge flicked the yo-yo neatly back into his cap. "Don't suppose any of you guys can handle the Riptide," he dared them.

"I'd like a go!" exclaimed Milo. "It's such a great … I mean *deep* yo-yo."

Smudge tossed the Riptide to Milo and flopped casually on to a rock to watch. Blot and Oscar draped themselves next to him.

Hooking the Riptide's string
over his flipper, Milo gave it
a spin. But it was much too
fast for him! It whizzed out,
flashing as it spun, then sped
back and bumped
him hard on the
nose!
Smudge and
Blot swayed with
laughter.
Poor Milo!
Little Dolphin and
Poppy rushed over
to him.
"I'm OK," he insisted, blinking
hard. "It doesn't hurt."

Little Dolphin could see that his friend's nose was very red. But he guessed Milo wouldn't admit it was sore in front of the squids.

Poppy picked some seaweed and put it on her head. "Hey, I have a *deep* cap too!" she announced. "Just like Smudge." She and Milo plonked themselves down next to the squids.

Little Dolphin didn't want to be left out so he swam over and perched next to Milo. But he soon found that lounging on a rock isn't easy when you don't have arms.

Just then, Vinnie the shark swam by. Little Dolphin saw his mouth drop open with surprise as he looked at the three wobbling dolphins.

"Hi, Vinnie!" drawled Milo. "Meet the new guys from Sandy Bay." He tried to wave a casual flipper and fell off the rock, on to his nose. Now it looked redder than ever!

Vinnie grinned, showing all his teeth.

"Want to be cool, do you?"
he said smoothly. "I've got just
the thing back at my cave. Fin
stickers with 'chill out!' written on
them. They're a bargain. They'll
only cost you—"

"Vinnie!" came a sharp voice
behind him, "I want a word with
you."

"Oh, no! It's that Hattie
again!" gulped Vinnie. "I'm off!"
With one flick of his tail he
disappeared round the reef.

Hattie the hermit crab arrived,
riding on an upturned bucket,
which was strapped to the back
of Fergal the turtle. "Did you see

where that pesky shark went?"
demanded Hattie. Her whiskers
quivered crossly. "He's been
selling things nobody needs – as
usual. He's just sold Fergal this
bucket and told him it's a shell
protector. I'm going
to get him a
refund!"

"Shell protector!" scoffed Blot,
looking at Fergal over his sunglasses.

"Silly turtle!" added Smudge. He nudged Oscar, who gave an embarrassed grin.

Poor Fergal turned bright pink and disappeared into his shell.

Hattie glared at Oscar and the two squids. Then she stared hard at Little Dolphin, Milo and Poppy. "What's the matter with you lot, wobbling on that rock like jellyfish?" she demanded. "You look really stupid. Come on, Fergal. Let's find Vinnie!" She tapped Fergal's bucket and Fergal swam away as fast as he could, with Hattie clinging on grimly.

Little Dolphin looked at Poppy and Milo. Maybe Hattie was right. They must all look very silly flapping their flippers as they tried to balance on the rock. But Little Dolphin wasn't going to say anything – he wanted to be cool and deep, like Oscar and his friends.

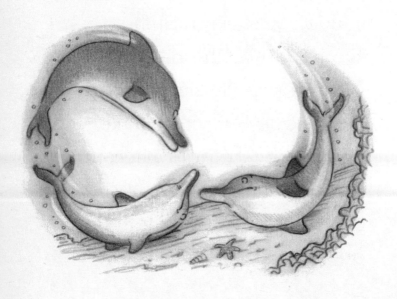

"I've got an idea," drawled Smudge, as he slid smoothly down to the sea-bed. "Let's play Roughball."

"Deep!" said Blot.

"Yeah," copied Oscar. "Deep!"

Little Dolphin whistled in alarm. "No! We're not allowed!" Only older sea creatures played that game, because it could be dangerous. Milo's big brother Frank played for the Urchin Bay Slammers, but he was almost grown-up.

"Not allowed?" scoffed Smudge. "Who says so?"

"All our mums," Little Dolphin said. "None of us are allowed to play."

Poppy and Milo nodded. Oscar didn't say anything, but Little Dolphin knew his mum wouldn't let him play either.

Smudge and Blot rolled their eyes at each other.

Little Dolphin decided he didn't care now if Smudge and Blot made fun of them. Roughball was dangerous and he didn't want anyone to get hurt.

"No point hanging around with a bunch of scaredy-shrimps, Blot, my friend," said Smudge.

"Too right!" agreed Blot.

"But I'll see you tomorrow, guys, won't I?" called Oscar anxiously as they turned to go.

"Sure," said Smudge. "See you tomorrow, Osc."

And the two squids swam away in a cloud of ink.

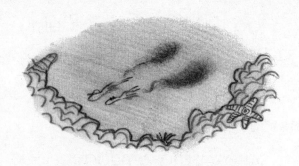

CHAPTER THREE

"Smudge and Blot are so *deep*," said Oscar as they watched the squids swim out of sight.

"Do you think they were joking about playing Roughball?" Little Dolphin clicked anxiously.

"Don't worry, Little Dolphin," chirped Milo. "We'll think of a different game that we can all play tomorrow."

"Let's play Sea Monsters!" squealed Poppy, spinning up and down. "We can meet at the old wreck tomorrow morning."

"Oh, yes!" agreed Oscar. "Sea Monsters is great!" Then he let his arms flop. "I mean *deep*," he said awkwardly. "I'll ask Smudge and Blot to come along!"

But when Oscar arrived at the old wrecked ship the next morning, he was on his own. There was no sign of Smudge and Blot.

"We can start the game now you're here, Oscar," Little Dolphin chirped brightly.

"I'll be the Monster of the Wreck."
He scooped up some long shells
with his mouth so that they stuck
out like big teeth.

   "I'll be the Dreaded
Flabberflop!" squeaked Poppy,
draping seaweed all over
herself and waving her flippers
menacingly.

"I'll be the Sand Serpent then," chirped Milo. "I'll bury myself in the sea-bed and you have to find me – unless I find you first!"

"Try not to get sand in your ears this time!" grinned Poppy.

Little Dolphin turned to Oscar. "Who are you going to be?" he asked.

But Oscar wasn't listening. He was looking at a yellow coral bush on the other side of the wreck. Little Dolphin peered at the bush.

Smudge and Blot were there, making ink rings in the water.

Smudge beckoned
to Oscar with
one of his long
tentacles.

"See you later,"
said Oscar,
sounding pleased.
And he swam off
to join them.

The Sea Monsters watched as
Smudge began juggling with some
conch shells.

"I thought Oscar had agreed
to play with *us*," exclaimed Milo,
sounding annoyed.

"We're just not *deep*
enough," said Poppy sadly.

"Never mind, we can still play with three!" chirped Little Dolphin. "Off you go, Milo."

Milo disappeared to hide.

Looking very fierce with his big monster teeth, Little Dolphin edged around the wreck.

Poppy the Dreaded Flabberflop followed. They glided silently along, nosing at the sand for signs of Milo the Sand Serpent. Where was he? Then they heard sounds from the other side of the wreck. They darted over.

"Got you, Milo!" whistled Poppy.

But it wasn't Milo. It was Smudge and Blot and they were teaching Oscar a new juggling game with brightly coloured pebbles. It looked such fun. They were so busy they didn't notice Little Dolphin and Poppy watching them.

"I wish I had arms to juggle with," sighed Poppy.

Milo's head popped up from the sand nearby. "Why have you stopped looking for me?" he spluttered, forgetting to be the Sand Serpent.

Then he saw Smudge, Blot and Oscar, who were now all making clever ink shapes in the water.

"Why can't they play things us dolphins can join in with?" he grumbled.

Little Dolphin spat out his Monster teeth. "Let's go!" he clicked. "Sea Monsters doesn't seem so much fun any more."

Poppy shook off her Flabberflop seaweed, and the three friends swam away from the wreck, leaving Oscar, Smudge and Blot doing high eights with each other.

Milo swished his tail crossly. "I wish Oscar had never made friends with those squids!" he clicked. "I don't think I'll ever speak to him again!"

CHAPTER FOUR

"What shall we play today?"
asked Little Dolphin, as he
bobbed in the waves with Poppy
and Milo the next morning.

"What about No Escape?"
suggested Milo. "There's an
empty cave by the clam beds.
It'll make a perfect prison."

No Escape was one of their
favourite games.

"But we need Oscar to be the Catcher for that," Little Dolphin reminded him. When Oscar was the Catcher, he used all his eight arms to block them and they had great fun trying to wriggle past him without being caught. They didn't escape very often!

"Oscar won't play," said Poppy sadly. "He just hangs round with Smudge and Blot, juggling or doing high eights or lounging on rocks – things dolphins can't do!"

"We *can* play without Oscar," said Milo firmly. "*I'll* be the Catcher."

"But how are you going to keep us prisoner?" chirped Poppy. "You haven't got any arms to catch us with."

"Flippers are just as good!" insisted Milo.

So they swam over the clam beds to the cave, and Little Dolphin and Poppy darted inside, to get ready to escape.

Then Milo tried to block the entrance. "You're my prisoners," he whistled fiercely. "There is no escape!"

Little Dolphin made a dart for the cave opening. Milo dived forward to stop him – and left a lovely big gap for Poppy to dash through! Milo spotted her and whirled round – so Little Dolphin saw his chance, and he escaped too!

Poor Milo. Whatever he did, Little Dolphin and Poppy kept escaping. And when Poppy spun towards him at top speed, he squealed and scurried off to try and hide with the clams!

"The Catcher's not supposed to be scared!" clicked Poppy, as she swam back into the cave.

"But I thought you were going to drill a hole in my belly!" complained Milo.

Little Dolphin slumped to the floor. "We're not having much fun, are we?" he said. The game wasn't the same without Oscar. A Catcher needed plenty of long arms.

"It's all Oscar's fault," grumbled Milo. "He brought those two squids to Urchin Bay."

Sadly, they set off for home, back over the clam beds and around the seaweed bushes. They steered well clear of Ragged Rocks, a place with nasty, sharp rocks that towered up from the sea-bed.

But as they passed, Little Dolphin saw someone playing in there. "Look!" he clicked.

Poppy and Milo stopped to look too.

"It's Smudge and Blot," clicked Poppy. "And Oscar!" Little Dolphin whistled in horror.

"They're playing Roughball!"

"But Oscar's too young!" whistled Milo. "My brother Frank's always coming home bandaged when he plays, and he's much older."

They watched anxiously. Smudge and Blot were on one team and Oscar was on the other.

Oscar didn't seem to be enjoying himself much. He was gripping the heavy ball tightly in one arm and swimming nervously towards his goal – a hole in one of the big jagged rocks.

Smudge suddenly leapt on him, tugging him down to the sea-bed. Then Blot barged in, shoved Oscar aside and grabbed the ball with one of his two long tentacles.

"Leave Oscar alone!" whistled Poppy. "That must be against the rules!"

"No, it's not," Milo told her. "It's a rough game."

Oscar picked himself up and chased after Smudge and Blot. The two squids had nearly reached their goal, tossing the ball from arm to arm. But as Smudge whacked the ball

towards the goal with a tentacle,
Oscar darted forward and
pushed the ball away. It was a
great save!

"Hurray!" whistled Poppy,
spinning with excitement.

"Well done, Oscar!" called Milo. Then he grinned. "Oops, I forgot I'm not talking to him!"

But the ball had smashed against the rock and loosened a big jagged boulder. It wobbled dangerously!

Little Dolphin could see that Oscar was right underneath and the boulder was going to fall. "Look out, Oscar!" he whistled in alarm.

It was too late. The boulder tumbled down with a terrible crash and Oscar was hit!

CHAPTER FIVE

Little Dolphin rushed over to
Oscar. Milo and Poppy followed
close behind.

Oscar was lying on the
sea-bed. There was a nasty cut
on one of his arms. "Ow! It
hurts!" he groaned.

"Poor Oscar!" squeaked
Poppy. "You're bleeding!"

Smudge and Blot took one look

and began to back away.

"That's bad, Blot," said Smudge anxiously.

"Yeah," replied Blot. "What are we going to do, Smudge?"

"Dunno," said Smudge. "The sight of blood makes me go all funny."

The two squids clung to each other and quivered.

Oscar turned to Little Dolphin, Poppy and Milo. "Can you help me to get home?" he pleaded. "I don't think I can swim."

Little Dolphin dabbed Oscar's wound with a piece of sponge. "Don't worry, Oscar," he clicked. "We'll get you home."

"But how?" squeaked Poppy.

"Oscar will be here for ever!" quavered Blot, tangling his arms into an anxious knot.

"He'll bleed to death!" whimpered Smudge, covering his eyes.

Little Dolphin ignored the silly squids and thought hard. "I've got it!" he whistled. "Milo and I will tow Oscar home. He can hold on to our fins. It'll be all right if we swim really slowly.

Poppy, you go and tell Oscar's mum we're on our way."

Poppy nodded then sped off.

Oscar wrapped an arm round each of his friends' fins, and gripped tightly with his suckers. "I'm ready," he said bravely.

Then Little Dolphin and Milo slowly towed Oscar away from Ragged Rocks, and towards his cave.

Next day, Little Dolphin, Milo and Poppy went round to visit their injured friend.

"My arm's much better now," Oscar told them. "Thank you for helping me home. I haven't seen Smudge and Blot at all."

"Perhaps they feel a bit embarrassed," Little Dolphin said. "They weren't much help yesterday."

"Never mind, Oscar," chirped Milo. "Come for a swim with us instead!"

Little Dolphin grinned. He was glad Milo had forgotten that he was never going to speak to Oscar again.

"Great!" said Oscar, with a big smile.

They all swam along the reef, darting in and out of the coral and chasing each other until they were dizzy. But then they heard a familiar voice.

"Osc, my friend!" It was Smudge. He was gliding over the sea-bed towards them – and Blot was right behind. The two squids looked very awkward.

"Sorry about yesterday, Osc," muttered Smudge. "Hope your arm's OK now."

"It's much better!" said Oscar. "Thanks to my friends here, I'm fine."

"Yeah," said Smudge shyly. "We weren't very good friends to you yesterday. We got you to play roughball ..."

"... and we didn't help when you got hurt," finished Blot.

"We just came to say sorry ..." said Smudge, twiddling his cap, "... to everybody."

"And we wanted to ask something," added Blot in a very small voice. "Could we play with you guys?"

Oscar looked at Little Dolphin, Milo and Poppy.

They all beamed. "Of course!" they replied.

Oscar waved his arms happily – and got himself into a terrible knot.

Everyone cheered and dived in to untie him, even Smudge and Blot.

They were still in a wriggling heap on the sea-bed when Hattie and Fergal came by.

"You all seem to be having proper fun again!" laughed Hattie. "That's a relief!"

"Where's your bucket ... I mean your shell protector, Fergal?" asked Poppy.

"Hattie got me a refund," said Fergal shyly, looking at Smudge and Blot.

"We shouldn't have laughed at you, Fergal, my man," said Smudge.

"Don't worry," smiled Fergal, going pink. "I did look silly!"

"Well, now we're all here together, what shall we play?" asked Poppy happily.

Smudge turned to Little Dolphin "Could I try having a ride on your back?" he asked. "Like Osc did when you towed him home?"

"Yeah," agreed Blot. "It looked like a really cool way to travel!"

"Hop on then, Smudge," Little Dolphin chirped.

"And I'll take you, Blot," added Milo.

"Deep!" Blot cheered.

"I'm not being left out," snorted Hattie, waving her claws. "Come here, Poppy." And she scrambled on to Poppy's back and clung on tightly.

Oscar and Fergal waved as Little Dolphin, Milo and Poppy swam around them.

Little Dolphin swam so fast that Smudge's cap whizzed off. "Don't stop!" called Smudge. "I'll get it later."

"This is dee-ee-eep!" called Blot as Milo leapt out of the water.

"I'm glad we're all playing together!" whistled Poppy. She began to spin with happiness.

"You're making me dizzy!" laughed Hattie, her whiskers waving wildly.

At last, the rides came to an end.

"What shall we play now?" asked Blot eagerly.

"Let's teach Smudge and Blot No Escape!" squealed Poppy.

"As long as I'm not the Catcher!" chirped Milo.

"Don't worry, Milo," said Oscar. "I'll be the Catcher." He smiled at Little Dolphin. "But first, I think we should play Flotsam and Jetsam!"

"*Deep!*" agreed Smudge and Blot.

And everyone cheered.